Marmaduke goes to Spain

Marmaduke goes to Spain

Elizabeth Chapman

pictures by Eccles Williams

HODDER AND STOUGHTON
LONDON SYDNEY AUCKLAND TORONTO

*For Simon, even though he is much too old
for these stories*

Contents

I
Marmaduke's exciting flight

Joe, who was Marmaduke's driver, was learning to play the guitar. He could play the piano quite well, which was a help, he said. Even then he had to spend quite a lot of time practising, which, when the weather was warm enough, he did in the garden of the house in Yorkshire where he and the old, red lorry had lived for a long, long time.

'He does look rather smashing!' thought Marmaduke, as he watched Joe with his left foot on a little stool, holding the guitar across his knee, and carefully plucking the strings.

'Hm! That's a rather melancholy but beautiful tune,' said Marmaduke rather carefully, as he wasn't really sure how to say 'melancholy', and it was usually Joe who said the big words.

Because of that Joe looked up in surprise, and he was pleased that Marmaduke had said just what it was, a sad but beautiful tune.

'It's Spanish,' he said. 'After all it's a Spanish guitar, so I'm playing Spanish music.'

'Perhaps you should wear a Spanish dress then,' said Marmaduke wickedly. 'You know, all frills and roses, and go to Spain, and dance the flamenco.'

He expected Joe to be either a bit cross or very amused, but he was neither. Instead he looked at Marmaduke thoughtfully.

'You know, that's an idea,' he said. 'Not the dress,' he added. He sounded a bit irritable, Marmaduke thought. 'You are a bit silly sometimes, Marmaduke. But about going to Spain. I've never been, and I'd like to go, and I've got some money saved, so how about it, *amigo*?'

'*Olé*,' cried Marmaduke. 'Really,' he thought. 'I'm not going to let Joe do all the Spanish words.'

So that was how Marmaduke and Joe came to be in an aeroplane on their way to Spain.

'It's too far to drive you,' Joe had said. 'We're getting rather old for that sort of journey.'

So there they were. Joe in a comfortable seat looking out of the window, and Marmaduke below with two brand new, very expensive cars which were to be delivered to two very rich Spanish gentlemen.

Marmaduke had flown before, so he was quite happy and comfortable, until, 'Oh golly!' he thought. The plane suddenly dropped like a heavy stone. It didn't drop very far, although it seemed to go on for quite a while. Even though it was flying straight on as usual, it was, thought Marmaduke, 'bashing him about a bit'.

The two expensive new cars tooted rather miserably. It was their first flight after all, and it *was* frightening.

'Never mind!' said Marmaduke, comfortingly and bravely. 'It's only a storm, I think. We're in good hands. At least I hope we are,' he muttered to himself. 'I suppose the pilot knows how to deal with storms. I do hope Joe is not too frightened.'

Joe was a bit, but, 'It's all right,' he said to the

rather upset old lady sitting next to him. 'It's only a storm. We're in good hands.'

'At least, I think we are,' he muttered to himself. 'I suppose the pilot knows how to deal with storms. I do hope Marmaduke is not too frightened.'

The two friends had been together so long that they sometimes thought the very same thoughts.

Suddenly they stopped being 'bashed about' as Marmaduke said, and the plane started to fly very smoothly.

'Well, thank goodness for that,' said Marmaduke comfortably. 'Soon be in Spain,' he said to the two expensive new cars. '*Olé*, and so on and so forth,' he added merrily.

But I'm afraid he wasn't merry for very long.

'Hello, ladies and gentlemen,' came the pilot's voice over the loud-speaker. 'Hm, he might say "lorry and cars" as well,' said Marmaduke.

'Now there's no need to worry,' went on the pilot.

'Which usually means there is,' grunted Marmaduke.

'But the very bad storm has damaged our

11

undercarriage ("that's the landing-wheels", explained Marmaduke to the two expensive new cars) and we shall have to land without them Please fasten your seat belts, and all will be well. It may be a bit bumpy, but don't worry.'

'Oh dear!' said Joe. 'Don't worry indeed! That means we'll have to land without wheels, and Marmaduke is at the bottom of the plane, and that means that the floor he's standing on will hit the ground first.'

Poor Marmaduke! He tried not to think of it as the plane flew lower and lower and nearer and nearer to the ground.

'Spanish guitar!' he grumbled, really trying to be brave. 'I wish I'd never said anything about

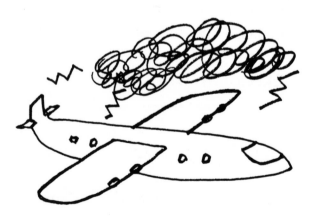

hat tune. Melancholy and beautiful indeed. Look where it's got us. About to flop down without wheels on to a Spanish airfield, and I bet it's all wet and skiddy with the rain.'

Lower and lower they flew. Joe thought of the green fields and dry-stone walls of home, and wished he'd never come. He looked out of the window. They were nearly on the ground. He held his breath, and the hand of the old lady next to him.

Marmaduke tried to stop shaking. His head-lamps made such a noise when he did, and the two expensive new cars were very frightened.

'It will be all right when it happens,' said Marmaduke brightly. 'Just like bumps-a-daisy.'

'I wish Joe were here with me,' he added to himself.

And then bump! bump! bump! slerrrrup! The plane skidded along the ground, shuddered a little as it twisted around, and then came to a stop.

'There!' said Marmaduke. 'We're down. I knew it would be all right.'

'Hello, Joe,' he said happily, as a short while

13

later the big doors of the plane opened, and the hot sun streamed in, followed by Joe with a smile right across his face.

'Happy landings and all that. *Olé* and hello *amigos*.'

2
Marmaduke makes marmalade

Joe drove to the nearest hotel for their first night in Spain. Their adventure had left both he and Marmaduke a little shaken, so after he had safely seen his lorry into a comfortable clean garage, Joe had a warm drink, to settle him down he said, and went to bed for a good night's rest.

Next morning was sunny and hot, and Marmaduke and Joe decided to take things quietly and explore the town. They drove gently through the winding streets and lanes between the old buildings, and admired the roses and the clematis growing in the courtyards between the houses.

'Oh look, Joe!' cried Marmaduke. 'Oranges! Growing on trees. Well, I never thought to see that. They look much nicer than just piled up in the green-grocer's at home.'

Joe stopped Marmaduke, and they sat and looked at the bright, round fruit hanging among the dark, glossy, green leaves.

'I wonder if they taste better when they're fresh,' said Joe. 'You know, like potatoes taste better straight out of the ground, and tomatoes just out of the greenhouse.'

'Ah yes,' said Marmaduke, rather naughtily. 'Just like the taste of oil straight out of the North Sea.'

'Making fun of me, are you?' said Joe, but not crossly. 'Well, I'll soon tell you about oranges, me lad. Look, there are a lot over there on the

road. Either they've fallen off someone's lorry, or they've fallen off the trees. Anyway, I'm sure no one will mind if I go and pick one up and taste it.'

Joe walked over, picked up an orange, then sat in the cab, peeled it and put a piece in his mouth.

'Delicious!' he said. 'Really, very delicious. Extraordinarily and wonderfully delicious!'

'Oh dear!' sighed Marmaduke, and giggled a little. 'Dear old Joe does sound funny at times.'

To his surprise he went on giggling. In fact he found he couldn't stop. He was probably suffering from the fright the storm had given him, and the dangerous landing of the aeroplane the day before. Delayed shock, the doctors call it.

'Ooooooooooooo, Joe,' he giggled. 'Dear me. I feel quite light-headed. Let's go and get some more oranges. Let's drive there.'

'He is a bit funny,' said Joe to himself worriedly. 'But never mind. I'll do what he wants.'

So Joe started up Marmaduke's engine, and began to drive him slowly down the road. Marmaduke giggled more than ever, and began to go quite quickly, and before Joe realised what

17

was happening, Marmaduke was 'bashing about' (as he had said of the aeroplane) among the oranges, squashing as many as he could.

'Tooooo-tooooot! Hurray!' he cried. 'I'm making marmalade. Fresh orange marmalade. Tastes much better than out of a jar. Extraordinarily and wonderfully delicious. Tooooot-toooooot!'

Joe by this time was very annoyed.

'Behave yourself, Marmaduke,' he said. 'Really! Come on now, let's get away from here. There's someone or something coming. Come

along now. We'll drive straight along, quietly please.'

What Joe had seen coming along the road behind them were horses. Sitting on the horses were men in black suits and big black hats, and girls in brightly-coloured dresses, with lots of frills. They were coming home from a fair and looked very pretty.

But unfortunately for Marmaduke, when the first horse put its hooves on the squashed oranges, it began to slip and slither and down it went on to the ground. Its two riders were soon rolling in the dirt.

'It's that stupid lorry,' yelled the Spanish gentleman riding behind the fallen animal. 'I saw him playing the idiot and squashing the oranges. After him!'

Marmaduke and Joe didn't understand what he was saying because they didn't know that much Spanish, but he sounded very angry, and was pointing his whip at them.

'OOOOOO, *Olé*!" muttered Marmaduke. 'I'm off.' And Marmaduke set off at top speed through the little streets.

'Slow down, Marmaduke,' puffed Joe. 'Slow down. These streets aren't wide enough.'

But Marmaduke could hear the sound of horses' hooves behind him, and had seen the whips, and was quite frightened.

'Toooot-tooooot! Tooooot-toooooooot!' he cried, as he dashed along the streets and out of the town.

'Oh!' he gasped, as he drove along the dusty country road with horses galloping behind him.

20

'It's just like Cowboys and Indians this is. Thank goodness they haven't any arrows.'

Then, 'Thump!' Marmaduke's left front wheel hit a big stone sticking up by the roadside, and Marmaduke came to a stop.

'Oh dearie, dearie me!' he said sadly. 'It looks as though I've been a very, very silly lorry.'

The first rider to reach them could speak a little English.

'You are from England?'

21

'Yes,' replied Joe unhappily.

'Then please come back to the town with us.'

Sadly the little procession went back down the country road and soon they came to the fallen horse and the squashed oranges.

'Perhaps his leg is broken,' said the Spanish gentleman. 'We will have to wait and see.'

Marmaduke and Joe waited dismally in the sunshine until the vet. and a policeman arrived.

The Spanish gentleman started talking to the policeman.

'Oh Joe,' said Marmaduke. 'Do you think he's talking about me?'

'Seems like it,' said Joe sharply. 'He's looking at you very angrily and the policeman is writing in his notebook, and also looking at you. What do you expect after the way you behaved?'

Then a lady came out of a nearby house, and came over to Marmaduke and Joe.

'Could I be of any help?' she asked. 'It looks as though you may be in trouble.'

'Oh Madam!' breathed Joe. He was so relieved. 'I do believe you're English. Oh madam! Yes please. We could do with some help.'

Help them she did. Not only was she an English lady, but a very clever lady as well. After she had listened quietly to Joe, who told her all about the storm, and the dangerous landing in the aeroplane, and Marmaduke giggling, and the making of the marmalade, she turned to the policeman, and smiled politely and began talking to him in Spanish. She talked about Marmaduke's very frightening time in the aeroplane, and delayed shock, and so on and so forth, and said that there was really nothing wrong with the horse, was there? She added that she was sure Joe would sweep up the squashed oranges. All the time she was smiling sweetly and politely at the policeman. He, poor man, was so over-whelmed and bewildered and enchanted by all this talking and smiling, that he quickly shook hands with the lady, then with Joe, gave Marmaduke a pat on his bonnet, and set off on his bicycle without a backward look.

The vet. said the horse wasn't hurt at all, and that it too would probably have delayed shock tomorrow, but he didn't think it would be a good idea for it to make any marmalade.

Then, after Marmaduke had apologised all round for the trouble he had caused, the English lady invited them all into her house for a cup of tea. Marmaduke stood in the road outside, and as she was closing the door, she gave the lorry a very big wink.

'Delayed shock indeed!' she said. 'High spirits more like.'

'Oh my!' said Marmaduke, and if it had been possible for a lorry to grin, he would have done. That was a lucky escape.'

3
Marmaduke and the bull-fight

Marmaduke and Joe liked the town where
Marmaduke had made the marmalade, so they
decided to stay there for another day.

'We don't need to rush,' said Joe. 'The English
lady says there are plenty of things to see here.'

'Yes,' said Marmaduke. 'I heard someone say
there was a bull-fight this afternoon, and that
everybody would be going to that.'

'Well, I don't think I want to go, Marmaduke.
Bull-fights have been going on in Spain for hun-
dreds of years, and most Spaniards seem to
enjoy them. There's certainly a lot of colour, and
jolly costumes, and all that, but I myself think it's
cruel. A man fights a bull and usually the bull gets
killed and sometimes the man gets injured, but
both the man and the bull have to be very brave.

and the people admire that. But no, I don't want to go.'

'So I don't either,' said Marmaduke cheerfully. 'Let's go and look at the cathedral instead.'

On their way to the cathedral that afternoon, they found themselves among quite a crowd of people all going to the bull-ring, which is like a very large circus ring surrounded by rows and rows of seats. They had to pass this on their way to the cathedral, and nearby they saw a little boy sitting on a bench with his head buried in his arms, crying bitterly.

Marmaduke stopped.

'Oh, Joe,' sighed the lorry. 'We can't ask him

what the matter is because we can't speak Spanish, but we can't leave him like that.'

Just then the English lady came walking down the road. She had been to a shop near the bull-ring to buy a new dress, and as soon as she saw Marmaduke and Joe she came over to greet them.

She was very kind and was careful not to say anything about Marmaduke's disgraceful behaviour with the oranges. After they had each said 'How are you?' and 'Very well thank you,' Joe drew her attention to the little boy who was still crying as though his heart would break.

'I will go and ask him what his trouble is,' said the English lady, and off she went.

She was soon back, holding him by the hand, while he mopped up his tears with her clean, white handkerchief.

'Well, it's all very sad,' she said. 'His uncle breeds fighting bulls, and also looks after a little black bull belonging to Pedro here, which isn't a fighting bull at all, but a gentle little animal who is Pedro's pet. By some dreadful muddle, the little black bull has got mixed up with the fighting bulls, and has been brought here to fight.'

'Oh Chico!' cried Pedro piteously. 'My little Chico!'

'Oh dear!' sighed the English lady. 'He will surely be killed.'

'Well, we can't have that, can we?' said Marmaduke briskly. 'We shall rescue him. Into the cab with you both. We've no time to waste.'

The English lady did not hesitate. Quickly she hustled Pedro into the seat beside Joe and then scrambled in beside him.

'Right!' said Marmaduke. 'Off we go. There's a wide entrance there I think, through those gates. Open them up, Joe, and we'll drive in.'

Before anyone knew what was happening, Joe had opened the gates, driven Marmaduke through, and closed them again. They were in a kind of road between the seats, and in front of them, on the other side of a high fence called a *barrera*, was the bull-ring. All the people were shouting and cheering at the bull-fighter, the *matador* as he is called. He certainly looked very handsome in his red and gold costume, waving his red cloak at the bull, trying to make the animal charge.

'Oh, Chico! Chico!' cried the little boy piteously.

For Chico it was, and the gentle little black bull was looking quite dazed. He didn't know why he was there, nor what it was all about, and he was very frightened.

'It's too late,' said the English lady sadly. 'The *matador* will soon draw his sword and Chico will die.'

'Not on your life he won't,' cried Joe, and like an English knight of old thought Marmaduke proudly, Joe jumped from the lorry, dashed through a little door in the *barrera*, and ran into the ring, where he caught hold of the *matador's* arm, and pulled him away from the terrified little bull.

Oh, what a noise there was! The crowd jumped to its feet and shouted angrily, two policemen ran into the ring, and began to pull Joe away, and Joe shouted at the top of his voice:

'It's Chico! It's not a fighting bull at all. Un-hand me I say. He shall not be killed.'

'Bravo!' cried Marmaduke. 'I say,' he said to the English lady, 'hadn't you better go and explain, or the next thing is we shall have Joe put in the ring to fight the bulls.'

'Well, I don't think it will come to that,' replied the English lady. 'But yes, you're right, I'd better join the party.'

So very calmly, and in a very dignified manner, the English lady walked across the ring, put up her hand to stop the policemen taking Joe away, and began to talk in her very pleasant, smiling way.

Everyone calmed down immediately and listened, and after they had listened, the policemen nodded their heads, the *matador* shook hands with Joe, and the English lady tied her long, silk scarf round the little bull's neck, and led him back to Marmaduke and the little boy.

Oh, how pleased Pedro was. Soon, he and Chico were in the back of the lorry, Joe opened the big gates, and Marmaduke drove out of the bull-ring and through the town into the country to Pedro's house.

His mother and father were looking out for him. They had been feeling worried, but when they heard the story they shook hands with the

31

English lady and with Joe, and patted Marmaduke's radiator, and said: '*Nuestra casa es su casa*', which means 'Our house is your house'. The Spanish people are very polite.

'*Gracias, gracias,*' they said over and over again, which is the Spanish word for thank you, and then asked the English lady if they would honour them by resting in their cool and quiet olive-grove, and later joining them in a meal.

So Marmaduke and Joe and the English lady spent the rest of the day very happily and quietly,

sitting amongst the olive-trees, and watching the little boy stroking his gentle, black bull.

'When the stars came out, the English lady and Joe and Pedro, and Pedro's mother and father and his two sisters, sat at a wooden table on the terrace outside the house, and ate *paella*. This is often eaten in Spain, and is made of rice coloured yellow with saffron, to which all sorts of nice things are added, chicken, and ham, and tomatoes, and green peppers, and peas, and beans, and sometimes shell-fish.

Joe ate every bit which was on his plate and said:

'Smashing, that was!' And then, bowing to Pedro's mother. '*Gracias, Señora.*'

Marmaduke, standing nearby, smiled fondly.

'Dear Joe!' he thought. 'Wherever we go, he always knows how to behave nicely.'

4
Joe has an accident

Joe did enjoy his *paella* with Pedro and his family, and Marmaduke enjoyed seeing Joe enjoying himself. That was not the end of the evening, however, not by any means. In fact, it might have been better if it had been.

As well as olive trees, Pedro's father had a small vineyard, and when the grapes were ripe on the vines, these were gathered and made into a wine called sherry. A great deal of sherry is made in southern Spain, and as they send a lot to England, Joe had drunk it before.

'I would like you to try my sherry,' said Pedro's father. 'See, I have a cask here all ready for you, and we will test the wine in the real Spanish way.'

Pedro's father fetched from the house a thin rod with a little silver cup at the end, which he let down into the cask. Then he drew up the wine in the silver cup and poured it into a glass which he was holding in his other hand. This he gave to the English lady to drink.

'Now, I will show you something,' he said to Joe, and he picked up six glasses in his right hand, and filled them in turn from the silver cup without spilling a single drop, which was very clever, as this is most difficult.

Everyone clapped and cried: 'Bravo!'

Then he handed the silver cup and six glasses to Joe.

'You try, *Señor*,' he said. 'And whatever you keep in the glasses you drink.'

'Oh well, that won't be much,' said Joe. 'What a shame though, if I spill all the sherry on the ground.'

So Joe was very careful. He slowly let down the silver cup on the thin rod into the cask, slowly pulled it up, and poured it into one glass. Then he had four glasses filled, and then he had five. Everyone raised their hands in amazement

36

at such cleverness, and said he would never, never be able to fill the sixth.

Then Joe began to get nervous and his hand began to shake, and just as he was filling the sixth glass, his hand began to shake more, and two of the glasses tipped over, and the sherry fell out.

'Oh, but that was very good,' smiled the English lady, as she helped him to put the four full glasses on the table. 'Now you must drink the sherry, or Pedro's father might be offended.'

So Joe drank one glass, and said: 'Very nice, yes, very nice indeed.' Then he drank another

glass and said: 'Absolutely delicious'. Then he drank another glass and said: 'Never have I tasted sherry with such a beautiful flavour.' Then he drank another glass and said: 'Absolutely sm-smashing!'

Oh dear! Four glasses of sherry is rather a lot all at once, and Joe was having a bit of trouble with his words. He was also feeling very happy and jolly, so he fetched his guitar from the front of the lorry, and shouted: 'Come on, we'll have a sing-song.'

So Joe sat in the back of Marmaduke, and started to play, but he didn't play one of his melancholy and beautiful Spanish songs, but instead he played a lively Spanish dance.

'Good gracious!' thought Marmaduke. 'Wherever did he pick that up?'

Then Pedro's two sisters began to dance, stamping their heels and twirling their skirts to the sound of the music.

'H'm!' said Marmaduke. 'I suppose that's what they call *flamenco* dancing. Very pretty, but I wish Joe would stop drinking the wine.'

For everyone kept on handing Joe wine from

other barrels to taste, and this went on for quite some time, until Joe got quite carried away, handed his guitar to Pedro to play, and then began to dance himself, on the back of Marmaduke of all places!

Stamp! Stamp! went Joe's heels on Marmaduke's back.

'*Olé! Olé!*' sang Joe at the top of his voice.

Stamp! Stamp! went his heels as hard as he could.

'Oh dear!' gasped Marmaduke. 'This is really very painful.' Then he became rather cross. 'Joe is being very silly,' he snapped to no one in particular, because everyone was busy singing and dancing. 'He's had far too much wine and should know better. Carrying on like this and making an exhibition of himself. I don't know what they would say at home, I really don't. One thing I am sure of, this sort of thing always ends in tears.'

And, of course, so it did, or as good as, for suddenly, in the middle of one great leap and a great '*Olé*', Joe lost his balance, and fell over the side of the lorry.

'Serve him right,' said Marmaduke crossly.

'Now perhaps we can go home and have some peace and quiet, although how he's going to drive me after all that wine, I don't know.'

Then Marmaduke stopped being cross and began to feel anxious, and everyone stopped dancing and singing, and, all at once, there was complete silence. For Joe had not got up from where he had fallen, and one leg was bent under him in a rather queer shape.

'Oh, Joe, what have you done?' sighed Marmaduke.

Pedro's father looked at Joe gravely. 'We must get him to hospital at once,' he said. 'Quickly,'

40

he said to his wife, 'fetch some blankets and we'll
ay him in the back of the lorry, and if Marma-
luke does not mind, I will drive him to the
hospital.'

The English lady explained all this to Marma-
luke, who, as he looked at Joe lying so still, felt
as though the world had stopped going round,
and that life was suddenly very frightening.

'Oh, if anything happened to Joe, I couldn't
bear it,' he moaned to himself, but at the same
time he knew he would have to.

Very gently, Pedro's father and mother and the
English lady lifted Joe into the back of the lorry,

and covered him with the blankets. All this time Joe didn't stir, and his eyes were closed.

Poor Marmaduke! Slowly and carefully Pedro's father drove him along the country road and the lorry had never felt so sad in the whole of his long life.

The English lady sat with Joe and tried to hold him still when the lorry jolted a little, which it did sometimes however careful Marmaduke was. Fortunately it wasn't far to the hospital, but Joe still had not stirred when the attendants gently lifted him on to a stretcher and took him into the hospital. Pedro's father and the English lady followed.

Marmaduke stood outside and waited. It was such a long wait, and Marmaduke thought sadly of the good times he and Joe had had together and he worried and worried and worried. Even when someone stopped and patted him, and said 'What a good old English lorry!' as happened whenever he went abroad, all he could do was say, 'Thank you,' as politely as he could, but very quietly. The people, sensing something was wrong, went away.

Then, just as Marmaduke thought he could bear it no longer, Pedro's father and the English lady came out of the hospital. It seemed to take ages for them to walk over to Marmaduke, but it didn't really, and soon the English lady was saying kindly:

'Well, it's not too bad, Marmaduke. Joe must have hit his head on a rock when he fell, and knocked himself out, but he has come round now, and is asking about you. The only trouble is that he has also given his ankle a severe sprain, which means he won't be able to drive for a day or two. The doctor says he has to stay in hospital tonight to recover from the shock, so we've told him that Pedro's father will let you stay at his place tonight.'

'Thank you,' said Marmaduke quietly, and then they all three drove away, and after they had dropped the English lady at her home, the other two rode off into the country.

Marmaduke felt tired with all the excitement and worry, but suddenly, he found that the world was going round again, and life was not frightening any more.

'Silly old Joe,' he smiled fondly. 'Drinking al
that wine, and then thinking he can dance flamenco at his age. Ah well, we all make mistakes
and I've made plenty in my time. Dear old Joe.'

5
Marmaduke gets stuck

Next morning Marmaduke wondered what they were going to do for the next few days as Joe would not be able to drive.

'I shall just have to sit here and look at the olive tree all day I suppose,' said Marmaduke glumly to himself.

He cheered up, however, when Pedro's father came out of the house and said he was going to drive him to the hospital there and then to fetch Joe.

They picked up the English lady on the way, and coming back to Pedro's house, they were a very jolly party indeed. The English lady, and Pedro's father had a long conversation in Spanish. At the end of this, the English lady said to Joe:

'Pedro's father and I have an idea, Joe. He has

a brother who owns a farm in the north of the country, whom he would dearly love to visit, but he has no car, and the trains are not very convenient. As you cannot drive, I wondered if you would like him to drive Marmaduke to the farm, and you as well of course, and I would go with you. I haven't seen that part of Spain, and I could help if you didn't understand his Spanish, and he didn't understand your English.'

Joe and Marmaduke thought this was a good idea, and as Joe was now feeling completely well, except for his ankle of course, they decided to set off next morning. Pedro would go with them too, but the rest of the family would have to stay at home to look after the vines. They didn't mind this as they had plenty of nice things to do at home.

The following morning, Marmaduke and Joe, Pedro, Pedro's father, and the English lady, set off very early indeed, as it was a good day's journey to the north of Spain.

'Tooooot-toooooot!' said Marmaduke, rather sleepily, as they drove along the country roads. 'I think we should sing our song, Joe, just to get

ourselves really awake. Anyway, we haven't sung
it for some time.'

So they sang:

> *'Merrily we go,*
> *Marmaduke and Joe,*
> *Singing high and low,*
> *Merrily we go.'*

Then Pedro tried to sing it, and got all the
words wrong, and in the end fell about the cab
laughing, and said: 'I *will* sing. Listen please!

> *Pedro he too go,*
> *And Marmaduke and Joe,*
> *Happy amigos,*
> *In España—a—a'*

47

but he didn't know how to finish it off and again fell about the cab laughing.

By this time, everyone was wide awake, and from then on, they had a happy time travelling through the Spanish countryside.

It was quite late when they got to the village where Pedro's uncle lived. In fact, it was already dark, and Marmaduke, being rather old, was exceedingly tired.

The English lady said: 'Now, I'm very sorry, Marmaduke, but I'm afraid we shall have to leave you in the village square. You see, the street where Pedro's uncle lives is too narrow for you to go through.'

'Go on!' said Marmaduke, a bit rudely, but he *was* tired. 'Pedro's father said he had a farm.'

'So he has,' said the English lady, 'but the farmers here don't have houses on the farm land. The village is built on a rocky hill, which is no use for farming, so they live in the village, and save all the good, flat land around the hill for farming.'

'Humph!' said Marmaduke grumpily. 'That's not what they do in England. Whoever heard of a farmer not living on his farm? Well, I'm not going to stand on my own all night in the square, and that's a fact. I'm going up the street with the rest of you.'

Joe sighed. He was tired too, as he wasn't young either, and after all he had been in hospital.

'Oh dear!' he thought. 'Marmaduke's being difficult.' But he supposed he must be weary and understood how he felt.

So Joe said: 'Well, let's try, and see if he can get up the street.'

'All right,' said the English lady. 'But I really think it is a waste of time. Anyway, we can but try. Here's the street, turn left here, Marmaduke, and go slowly.'

Marmaduke turned left but the road was rough and steep.

'It has to be rough,' explained the English lady. 'Because a lot of people here get about on mules and horses, and if the roads were smooth, their hooves would slip, and they might fall down.'

'Humph!' Marmaduke grunted again. 'Might be all right for the mules and horses, but I'm

49

tired of this rough road. I'm going to go quickly and get it over with. Brummmmm! Hold tight, everyone, up we go.'

Up they went indeed, for a few yards, and then: 'Crunch! Screech! Scrape!' Marmaduke came to a sudden stop. He was stuck in the narrow street, with each front mudguard firmly wedged into the house at each side.

Most people were having their evening meal, and when they heard the noise, doors and win-

dows flew open, and heads popped out, and soon there was a chattering and chirping just like a lot of sparrows, Joe thought.

The English lady didn't say: 'There, I told you so,' as she might well have done, but sat quietly wondering what to do.

'At least there's plenty of light from the open doors and windows,' she said. 'But we can't do anything. We're so wedged in that we can't get out of the lorry.'

'Oh dear!' sighed Marmaduke. 'Silly again. That's me. Sorry!'

Two strong-looking men came out of the nearest house, and tried to push Marmaduke backwards, but he didn't move. Then someone tied a horse on to the back of him, and the horse pulled and pulled and pulled, until Marmaduke felt as though his back would leave his front, and began to get quite worried, but still he didn't move. He was well and truly fixed on the walls.

Then Pedro's father saw his brother coming down the road, and when the brother saw who it was in the lorry, he threw up his hands in delight.

'Ah, welcome, welcome!' he cried. 'How lucky you are to travel in this fine old, English lorry. But what are you doing standing here, my friend?' he asked, placing his hand in a very friendly fashion on Marmaduke's bonnet.

'What does he say?' asked Marmaduke rather irritably. He was very tired indeed. So the English lady spoke in English and told Marmaduke and Joe what he had said, and then spoke in Spanish and explained to the Spanish gentleman that they were stuck, very stuck, stuck there for ever in all probability.

The Spanish gentleman said something which Marmaduke thought must be the Spanish for 'Oh dear!' His face looked like that anyway.

Then Joe, who had been carefully examining the houses on each side, had one of his famous ideas.

'I think,' he said slowly. 'I think that if I'm not mistaken these houses get closer to the street the higher up they go, if you see what I mean. What I mean is that the bedroom windows are almost hanging over the top of us, whereas the front steps are farther away from the bits of the walls on which we are stuck. Now, Marmaduke, you may not like this, but I think – er – yes – I think . . .' Everyone held their breath wondering what was coming next. 'Yes, I am sure.' And he began to speak firmly and not so slowly. 'If we let down all your tyres, Marmaduke, then you will sink down nearer the ground, and because your mudguards will then be lower down, they shouldn't catch on the walls, and we can then run backwards a few feet.'

The English lady and Pedro and Pedro's father looked at Joe with much admiration.

'Oh well!' said Marmaduke. 'If it's the only way. Serves me right anyway.'

Pedro's father told his brother the plan, and the brother let the air out of the front tyres, and shouted to a man standing behind Marmaduke to let the air out of his back tyres.

'Wheeeeeeesh!' went the tyres. Marmaduke sank down on to his rims, and the mudguards came off the walls.

Joe gave a sigh of relief. He hadn't been really absolutely, perfectly sure that his plan would work, but all was well. Pedro's father took off the handbrake, and let Marmaduke slide back a few feet.

'There now,' he said. 'We can pump you up again, and back you down to the square.'

But, do you know? no one had a pump, so, in the end, Marmaduke just *had* to stay there all night, near to Joe and his friends at Pedro's uncle's house.

'There, all's well that ends well,' said Marmaduke cheekily, as Joe said good-night to him.

'You are very wicked, Marmaduke,' said Joe, but he smiled fondly at him all the same.

6
Marmaduke speaks Spanish

The following day, Marmaduke was woken very early, as the men set off for the fields at about six o'clock. Most of them went on mules or in little horse-drawn carts called *carretas*, which were kept in the court-yards of the houses. Pedro's father had been up at five o'clock, because he had to find someone with a pump, so that Marmaduke could be moved out of the way. Luckily he found one, and an hour later the lorry was comfortably parked under the trees in the village square.

Marmaduke enjoyed being there, watching everyone set off for their day's work, and gave a very cheerful 'toot-toot' to Pedro and his cousin, Carlos, as they passed by with the flock of sheep belonging to Pedro's uncle. Carlos had a lonely job. He was his father's shepherd, and each day he took the flock of seventy-three sheep from his house to the fields, so that they could eat the grass there. He watched over them until the middle of the day, when he brought them back home to their pen in the court-yard of the house. It is so hot in Spain in summer that everyone has a rest in the shade – a *siesta* it is called – when the sun is hottest in the afternoon, and the sheep were always glad to get back home out of the fierce heat.

So, because it was such a lonely job, Carlos was really glad to have Pedro's company.

At about ten o'clock, Joe came hobbling down the street and into the square. Pedro's father was with him, and he was carrying a large basket. Inside it was some ham and sausage, with large hunks of bread, and green olives. Also a bottle of wine.

'We are taking this to Pedro's uncle and the boys,' explained Joe.

'What, so early?' exclaimed Marmaduke. 'It can't be long since breakfast. I thought boys shouldn't eat between meals.'

'They haven't had any breakfast,' said Joe.
'They have a large meal late at night, and that
sees them through until ten o'clock in the morning. They usually take it with them at six o'clock,
but we thought we would like to go and see them,
and said we would bring the food.'

So Joe and Pedro's father climbed into Marmaduke's cab, and off they went.

It was already very hot, but soon they heard
the gentle tinkle-tinkle-tinkle of lots of little bells,
and there was a flock of sheep. One in every six
sheep had a bell fixed to its collar, and this helped
to keep the flock together. And very nice music
too, thought Marmaduke.

Then they heard another sound – clickety-
click, clickety-click, clickety-click'.

'Ah, I know what that is,' grinned Joe. 'It's
castanets. They hold them in their hands, and

click them in time to the music when they're doing their *flamenco* dancing.'

'And we don't want any more of that from you, thank you Joe,' said Marmaduke, pretending to be severe.

Pedro had brought a pair of *castanets* as a present for Carlos, who was sitting on a rock practising while Pedro clicked his heels and clapped his hands in real *flamenco* fashion, which, the way they do it, makes a very loud clap indeed. They each had one eye on the sheep, but their two sheep-dogs, who were mother and daughter, were doing their work well and watching all the time to make sure the flock kept together.

Pedro's father drove Marmaduke to the vegetable plot where his brother was working, gave him his share of the food, and then came back to the boys, as he had said that he would give a hand with looking after the sheep.

They all sat happily under a tree eating the bread and ham and sausage, and drinking the wine. Afterwards Pedro began to play a tune on his tin whistle, and Carlos practised his *castanets* and his heel-banging, while Joe rested his ankle,

and Pedro's father kept both eyes on the flocks. There were no walls or hedges to the fields, so it was important that the sheep did not stray.

Then, all at once, Pedro's father got up and walked over to the sheep. He bent down and picked something up in his arms, and walked back. It was Bella, the mother sheep-dog. He put her gently down in the shade of the tree.

'She's not well by the look of things,' said Joe. 'Oh, I wish the English lady had come with us. We need a bit of explaining, so that we know what to do. Oh goodness!' he exclaimed. 'Look at the sheep.'

Marmaduke looked, and Joe shook the shoulder of Pedro's father to attract his attention, and pointed to the flock. Bella's daughter was too young to have been properly trained in sheep-minding, and with Bella gone, the animals had started wandering. Some were going one way, some another, some another, bells were tinkling, but somehow it didn't sound like music any more, the sheep were baaaing like anything – they were very confused – and Pedro and Carlos were running from one part of the flock to the other, quite as confused as the sheep.

Pedro's father leapt into the lorry, and Joe stumbled in after him.

'We go,' he cried. 'Men. Get men. The crops.'

'I think he means we must fetch some men to collect the sheep, or they'll get into the wheat and barley and what not,' explained Joe to Marmaduke. 'Hm,' thought Marmaduke. 'Joe really must think I'm quite stupid. Of course that is what he meant. Anyway, off we go.'

And off they went, very quickly down the rough road. As they went Marmaduke hooted as loudly as he could, to attract the attention of the men working in the fields, and Joe stuck his hand out of the window, and pointed in the direction of the flock.

Soon men were running from all directions to cross the fields, and Pedro's father turned Marmaduke back the way they had come. Then, just

as they were passing a large and wonderful field of glowing, beautifully golden wheat, about forty sheep ran from the field on Marmaduke's right across the road to the field on his left.

'They'll break it down,' gasped Joe. 'That's what they'll do. Pedro's uncle will be ruined.'

'Oh, no, they won't,' said Marmaduke, and quickly he put himself between the wheat and the sheep, and stopped.

'Tooot-tooot!' he shouted. '*Olé, amigos, gracias, paella, flamenco . . .*

And would you believe it? the sheep stopped. They were so surprised, and again bewildered, like they were when Bella stopped looking after them. This time, however, instead of running in all directions, they just stopped, and began munching the green grass at their feet.

In a few minutes, the men arrived, and took them back to their pasture. Bella had recovered. She was really getting too old for the job, and the heat had made her feel quite odd. However, she and her daughter, who was rather in disgrace, as she should have done a little better than she did, gathered the sheep together, and they all went back home for an early *siesta*.

'Why they don't build walls round their fields like they do in Yorkshire I'll never know,' said Marmaduke to Joe later. 'Still, they know what's best, I suppose, but we should have been saved all this to-do if they did. I think, though, I must have quite a way with sheep,' he added importantly.

Joe agreed with him, but thought privately that if a large, red, noisy thing suddenly stops in your path, shouting a lot of words which add up to a load of nonsense, then you do stop.

'Still, never mind,' he thought. 'He wasn't afraid to risk looking silly, and it certainly worked.'

7
Marmaduke's spooky evening

Marmaduke and Joe and their friends had a lovely time on the farm, but soon it was time to leave. Joe's ankle was better by this time, so he was able to drive Marmaduke.

They left the village at six o'clock one morning, when everyone was setting off for work, so they had quite a good send-off, with everyone waving and calling 'Goodbye'. While she had been staying in the village, the English lady had taught everyone to say that.

It was a hot day, and Marmaduke was quite glad when at last they pulled into a small hotel. The first thing Joe did was to pour a large can of cold water into Marmaduke's radiator, and then he parked him under a large tree, while he and the others went into the hotel for dinner.

It was cool and quiet under the tree, and Marmaduke felt very rested by the time Joe came out to see him. It was already dark, and Marmaduke felt quite lively, even though he had had quite a long journey.

'What about a little run, Joe?' he asked. 'Just you and me. Might help to settle all that *paella* you've just eaten.'

'Well, actually, Marmaduke,' said Joe. 'It wasn't *paella*. We had some cold soup called *gazpacho*, then some fried sardines, and then some fruit. The soup was quite delicious, and I'm going to make some when I get home.'

'Oh dear! It's his important-sounding voice again,' sighed Marmaduke. 'I don't know what gets into him sometimes. Anyway, cold soup indeed! What good is that going to be in a Yorkshire winter?'

'Yes, Marmaduke,' Joe went on. 'I'll take you for a little run. It's very pleasant in the cool of the evening.'

'He's had a glass of wine,' muttered Marmaduke. 'Or two, I'm sure of it. *That's* when he gets his important voice.'

However, soon they were driving happily along the country roads. Sometimes they grumbled about each other, but they were good, old friends, and a little grumble or two didn't matter.

It was very hilly country, and there were no lights, so they had to watch carefully where they were going.

'I-it's rather d-dark, isn't it Joe,' whispered Marmaduke.

'Why is he whispering?' Joe asked himself. 'There's no one about to hear anything. Just hills and rocks. I'll ask him.'

So he did.

'I don't know,' Marmaduke replied in a very low voice. He tried to speak up but somehow he couldn't. 'I think it's because it's all a bit spooky.'

'Spooky!' exclaimed Joe. 'That means you think there might be ghosts and things? That's nonsense, Marmaduke. There are no such things as ghosts. Look, we'll stop here on this bridge, and just sit together in the dark for a little while,

and you'll see there's nothing at all to be afraid of.'

So Joe brought Marmaduke to a stop on a little hump-backed bridge over a stream. The water made a friendly sound as it gurgled and splashed over the stones in the bed of the stream, and they could hear some goats talking to each other in a field nearby.

'It's a pity they're Spanish goats,' said Marmaduke after a while. 'I should like to hear what they are saying.'

Joe said: 'One is probably saying, "I thought I heard a lorry coming and now I can't, and I think it's spooky," and the other is probably saying

"That's nonsense. There are no such things as ghost lorries."'

Marmaduke laughed. He wasn't afraid any more. The sound of the stream was so comforting, and the goats sounded very friendly.

'You're right as usual, Joe,' he said. 'There aren't any ghosts, only goats.'

Joe started up the lorry, and off they went, Marmaduke clanking and clattering with laughter.

'I know, Joe,' he said. 'I'll give them a toot, and then they'll know I'm real.' And he laughed a lot more.

'Hm, it's not that funny,' thought Joe. 'Still, it's cheered up the old boy, and that's the main thing.'

So: 'Tooooot-tooooooooot – i – tooooooot!' called Marmaduke. 'Hello, you ghosts, I mean goats. I'm not a ghost either, I'm a lorry from England. My name is Marmaduke and my driver is Joe. Toooot-tooooot. *Adiós amigos.*'

There's no knowing what the goats thought about this. However, they replied cheerfully enough in a long string of Spanish words. They too finished off with *adiós amigos,* so they really must have decided that Marmaduke was not a ghost. Perhaps they had never even thought it.

'Friendly chaps, aren't they?' said Marmaduke. 'Very nice chaps indeed, I'm sure. That is if we could have seen them. But then, you never can see ghosts can you, Joe?' he added wickedly.

Marmaduke had certainly got over his spooky feeling.

'I'm feeling what Charlie Brown's mother at home calls "high-spirited"', he told Joe. 'I shall now sing.'

And sing he did.

> *'Merrily we go,*
> *Marmaduke and Joe,*
> *Singing high and low,*
> *Marmaduke and Joe.*
>
> *We have seen no ghosts,*
> *In the Spanish dark,*
> *But we've heard some goats,*
> *Isn't it a lark?'*

'My word!' thought Joe. 'Two verses indeed. He *must* be feeling high-spirited. Still, that was a good effort, Marmaduke,' he said out loud. 'You are quite a poet as well as a singer.'

'Oh, go on,' chuckled Marmaduke. 'I'm just a daft old lorry.' But he was pleased with what Joe had said.

'Now, we'll just go over the top of this hill,' said Joe. 'And then we'll turn back.'

'Right-ho,' said Marmaduke cheerfully.

Marmaduke went up the hill in fine style for an old lorry who had done quite a lot of travelling. Then, just as they got to the top, the moon came out from behind another hill, and everything before them could be seen in the calm, eerie light.

'Oh, Joe,' breathed Marmaduke excitedly, 'do you see what I see? All those chimney pots sticking out of the rocks, and those doors in the hillsides. No houses, Joe. No cottages, or flats, or hotels, or castles. Just chimney pots and doors. It's pixies and goblins and such like who live here. I know about them. Charlie Brown at home told me. Told me all about them he did. And some are wicked. Come on, Joe, let's go. They'll put spells on us if they see us.'

Marmaduke was really frightened now. There were certainly chimney pots sticking out of the ground, and doors in the hillside, and everything was very quiet and weird-looking in the moon-light.

'Now, it's all right, Marmaduke,' said Joe in his soothing voice. 'There are no such things as goblins and pixies either. There must be some explanation.'

'Hum, there may be no pixies and goblins in England,' said Marmaduke. 'But you never know in a foreign country.

'Don't be silly, Marmaduke,' said Joe quite sharply. He was a little frightened too, because he couldn't understand what he was seeing, and things you can't understand sometimes are frightening.

'We're not running away,' he said firmly. 'We'll stay here a while, and perhaps all will be explained.'

So there they stood, but Marmaduke didn't like it. He didn't like it at all.

'Look at the smoke coming out of the chimney pots, Joe,' he whispered. 'They make noxious

71

brews in saucepans Charlie Brown says. They'll pro-probably come and pour one into my radiator.'

'Hush!' said Joe, comfortingly he hoped. He didn't know what else to say, as he didn't know what a 'Noxious brew' was.

Then – Creeeeek-eeeee-creeeeeeeeeek! In the hillside near to Marmaduke and Joe a door started to open.

'Ooooooooooooooooo,' trembled Marmaduke. 'It's a Spanish goblin. It is. It is.'

Slowly, slowly, creaking, and creaking, the door opened, and then – out stepped a perfectly ordinary Spanish lady and gentleman, who

aised their hands in friendly greeting to the two
riends, and disappeared into another door in the
opposite hillside.

Marmaduke and Joe turned round and drove
back to the hotel.

'Still can't understand it,' muttered Marmaduke. 'Perhaps goblins look like ordinary people
anyway.'

'All will be explained,' said Joe calmly. 'We
will ask the English lady.'

And of course, all *was* explained. The lady and
gentleman they had seen were gipsies, who, in
olden days, used to travel all over Spain, but now
many of them live in caves in the hillsides.

'Very nice places they are too, some of them,'
said the English lady. 'Just like your house I
expect, Joe, with nice furniture, and electric
light, and telephones.'

'There, you see!' said Joe, as he put Marmaduke
away for the night in the hotel garage. 'Even
goblins and pixies have arm-chairs and reading-
lamps, Marmaduke.'

'Now you're being silly, Joe,' smiled Marmaduke. 'Fancy thinking that I believed that those

creatures would be living there. I was only trying to stop you using your important-sounding voice, Joe.'

'Oh, well, it was a bit strange,' said Joe. 'And I know you really knew all the time that ordinary people lived there.'

'Oh, Joe is kind,' thought Marmaduke, as the garage doors closed, and his friend went away to bed. 'He knows quite well that I was frightened and really thought there might be goblins and pixies there, but he doesn't want to make me feel silly. But wait until I get home and tell Charlie Brown,' he chuckled to himself. 'We'll have what Joe calls "a real good laugh". I'll tell him about the ghosts and the goats too. That should make him laugh all the more. Really, all in all we've had a very spooky evening.'

8
Home again

Marmaduke and Joe very much enjoyed the rest of their holiday in Spain, but all good things come to an end, and the day came when they had to set off for home.

Joe drove Marmaduke to the airport, and after many cries of '*Adiós amigos*', and smiles and waves, the lorry and his driver were soon in their aeroplane, and flying away from Spain, back to England.

They had a good journey, and after landing at the airport in England, in no time at all, or so it seemed to Marmaduke, he and Joe were driving through their beloved Yorkshire countryside towards home.

It had been very, very hot in England while they had been away. In fact, it had been very,

very hot before they had left, and now there had been no rain for many weeks, and everywhere was very dry.

'Why, all the grass has turned from green to brown, Joe,' exclaimed Marmaduke. 'And a lot of the flowers and shrubs in people's gardens have died, and my goodness, doesn't everyone look hot!'

'Well, it is hot,' said Joe. 'Hotter than it was in Spain, and that's really quite strange.'

'Never mind, let's get home quickly,' said Marmaduke. 'It will be cooler on the hills.'

When they got to the hills it was cooler, for there was a pleasant breeze.

'That's better,' said Joe thankfully. He leaned out of Marmaduke's window, so that the breeze could blow on the bald patch on the top of his head. This bald patch became very hot in the sun, and the breeze cooled it down nicely.

Soon they dipped down into a wood, and it was very comfortable amidst the trees.

Then Joe sniffed, and sniffed again.

'I think I can smell burning, Marmaduke. I wonder . . .' But before he could say, 'I wonder

if there's a fire somewhere', they had driven out of the wood into a big cloud of thick smoke.

'Oh, Joe!' cried Marmaduke. 'The moors are on fire. Look, both sides of the road. Let's get back into the wood.'

Joe looked at the flames each side of them, and felt a little frightened, but he knew he had to make one of his decisions.

'No, Marmaduke,' he said at last, firmly. 'We can't do that. The trees will catch fire in no time, and then we shall have them crashing down on us. Best press on.'

So press on they did, through the hot, choking

smoke, and the dry crackling heather, burning with big orange flames.

'I know where to go, Marmaduke,' Joe said, trying to sound calm. 'Now don't panic, old friend, and I'll get you there, and then we shall be safe.'

'Don't panic indeed,' thought Marmaduke. 'My tyres are red hot, and my paint's blistering, and if my petrol gets a spark in it, then up we go to join the spacemen.'

In the midst of all the danger, he suddenly realised that was a funny thought to think, and as he said: 'Any minute now, five, four, three, two, one, zero, off we go', he felt much braver somehow, as of course they didn't go up. In fact, while he had been thinking these thoughts, Joe had taken him to where he had promised to take him, into the cool, cool, wonderfully cool waters of a big, but fortunately shallow lake.

'Oh, Joe, how clever you are,' sighed Marmaduke.

'I haven't finished being clever yet, Marmaduke,' said Joe briskly, as he jumped out into the water, grabbed two empty cans from Marma-

78

duke's back, emptied Marmaduke's petrol into them, and then lowered them into the water.

'And how, may I ask, am I to get home?' asked Marmaduke politely.

'We'll solve that when the time comes,' replied Joe. 'In the meantime, we don't want any trouble. We're quite safe now.'

The two friends stayed in the lake, and watched the fire burning all around them.

Then plop! Something had hit Marmaduke's back, but softly. Then another, plop!

Joe looked round through the back window.

'My goodness!' he said. 'It's two birds. Better go and see.'

So out Joe got again to have a look, and sure enough, it was two grouse from the moors, their brown feathers singed with the fire, and looking very tired. Joe took a cup from his cab, filled it with water from the lake, and gently bathed their feathers, and dribbled a little into their beaks.

Marmaduke felt a scratching on his back wheel.

'Quick, Joe,' he called. 'Someone else I think. Nearside back.'

And sure enough, there was someone there, a whole family of hares. They too looked very tired after running away from the flames.

'Knew it was you,' panted Father Hare. 'Recognised you I did. Knew you'd be in a safe place. Swam for it, we did. Look after the little ones, there's a good chap.'

So Joe lifted the family up into the lorry, where they lay tired but safe.

But other people had recognised Marmaduke and Joe, as they ran for their lives from the burning heather.

'Welcome home, Marmaduke and Joe,' cried Mrs Sheep, as she scrambled aboard, with Joe's help, as she wasn't very nimble. 'Rather too warm a welcome I'm afraid.'

Then a skylark flew down, and perched on Marmaduke's radiator, then another, then another, until there was quite a flock of them.

'Had to leave our nests in the heather,' they gasped. 'But the chicks are reared, and we're so glad to see you, Marmaduke and Joe.'

A squirrel came. He'd run right down the road through the woods. Then some field-mice, and a

pair of owls, and some blackbirds, and thrushes
and sparrows.

'Oh, I've never been a zoo before,' giggled
Marmaduke. 'What a lark!'

The skylarks thought he was being funny
when he said 'What a lark', and twittered and
laughed, and everyone joined in, and Mr Grouse
smoothed Mrs Grouse's feathers with his beak,

and said: 'There, there, my dear, everything's all right now.'

In fact, they all began to feel very happy suddenly. They had been through danger, they had found safety, and they were with friends.

Soon a lot of men arrived, and began beating the flames with large shovels to smother the fire. The breeze had died down now, so this wasn't spreading so much.

Then up the road to the lake, they heard the 'hoooo–ooooo–oooo' of a siren. It was the fire-engine, and in a short while the firemen were squirting the water from the lake through their hoses on to the flames.

'Don't take it all,' called Marmaduke wickedly. 'It's been a great friend to us.' As though they could.

Finally, the last little orange flicker had died down, the smoke had gone away, and there, all round them was the blue sky and the blue water. The skylarks looked at the sky, and rose in a cloud up into the air, singing as though their grateful hearts would burst with joy.

'Goodbye, Marmaduke and Joe,' they sang, as

they flew away, and 'Thank you.' In the same way, went the owls and the blackbirds and the thrushes and the sparrows and the grouse.

'Er, we'll stay with you for a while if you're going anywhere,' said Mr Hare. 'I don't think this hot heather will be nice for soft paws. Perhaps if we can go along with you, we might find some green fields, or at least this year, brown green fields, if you see what I mean.'

The squirrel thought he'd do the same, and Mrs Sheep, and after Joe had borrowed some petrol from the fire-engine and put it into Marmaduke's tank, they backed out of the lake, and drove off.

They found a field which was more green than brown, so off the hares went.

'Thanks most awfully, Marmaduke and Joe,' said Mr Hare. 'See you soon I hope.' Mrs Sheep went with them.

Then they found a clump of trees for the squirrel, soon Marmaduke and Joe were home.

'Oh, how nice it all looks,' sighed Marmaduke contentedly. 'I'd rather be here than up with the spacemen.'

'What is he talking about?' Joe asked himself. 'He must be suffering from heat-stroke.'

But Marmaduke was all right, though he did want to know how the fire might have started.

'Well, someone could have dropped a lighted match, or a burning cigarette end,' said Joe. 'Silly thing to do at the best of times, but when the grass is so dry, it's downright wicked.'

'Oh well!' sighed Marmaduke, as Joe put him into his nice, cool garage for the night. He was very tired after all the excitement. 'It was a good home-coming in a way – once we were safe. Good-night, dear Joe, *olé*, *gazpacho*, *paella*, and all that, and *gracias* for a lovely holiday.'

MARMADUKE THE LORRY
MARMADUKE AND JOE
RIDING WITH MARMADUKE
MARMADUKE'S GREAT DAY
MERRY MARMADUKE
MARMADUKE AND HIS FRIENDS
MARMADUKE AND THE ELEPHANT
MARMADUKE AND THE LAMBS
MARMADUKE GOES TO FRANCE
MARMADUKE GOES TO HOLLAND
MARMADUKE GOES TO AMERICA
MARMADUKE GOES TO ITALY
MARMADUKE GOES TO SWITZERLAND
MARMADUKE GOES TO MOROCCO